Gilles Gauthier

Mooch Gets Jealous

Illustrations Pierre-André Derome

Translation by Sarah Cummins

Formac Publishing Company Limited
Halifax, Nova Scotia 1993

Copyright © by les éditions de la courte échelle inc.

Translation copyright © 1993 by Formac Publishing Company Limited

Canadian Cataloguing in Publication Data

Gauthier, Gilles, 1943-

[Babouche est jalouse. English]

Mooch Gets Jealous

(First novel series)

Translation of: Babouche est jalouse.
ISBN 0-88780-217-6 (pbk.).   ISBN 0-88780-218-4 (bound)

I. Derome, Pierre-André, 1952- . II. Title. III. Title: Babouche est jalouse. English. IV. Series.

PS8563.A858B3213   1992   jC843'.54   C92-098705-2
PZ7.G38Je 1992

Formac Publishing Company Limited
5502 Atlantic Street
Halifax, N.S. B3H 1G4

Printed and bound in Canada.

Table of Contents

1
Maggie, oh Maggie

Maggie, magnificent Maggie, magical Maggie, Maggie, Oh Maggie.

Maggie is the most beautiful name on earth, in the heavens, and over the seven seas. There's no name more majestic, and no girl finer than Maggie.

There isn't a girl who is stronger, either. And if there's one guy who knows that now, it's Gary. Gary the clown, who used to spend all his time making fun of me.

Maggie has put him in his place. No two ways about it.

Gary didn't look like such a big shot when Maggie grabbed him by the collar and held him up against the wall, his feet dangling in the air. He couldn't even talk. Usually he's blabbering on, but he couldn't get a word out.

Gary was scared. It's the first time I've ever seen him like that. He was more scared of Maggie than I am of him. And that's saying something.

He turned as white as a sheet. His friends, Sebastian and Anne-Marie, were even paler than he was. They looked like ghosts.

I should mention that Maggie is not an ordinary little girl. She is taller than my mother, Judy. She towers over me, three heads taller.

I look like a flea next to her. Gary, who is not exactly short, looks like a dwarf.

And they say she's only twelve years old!

I think she forgot to count some of her birthdays. What will she be like when she grows up?

One thing for sure, she's not afraid of anyone at school. She owns the schoolyard. It's hers.

And in Maggie's schoolyard, there's only one boss: Maggie.

With her long red braids, she looks like a Viking. A Viking in blue jeans. She almost looks like a grown-up.

And you know what? She told Gary that he better leave me alone unless he wanted to mess with her.

She mentioned it just when he was twisting my arm to make me give him a chocolate bar I had in my lunch.

Gary froze and let go of my arm. He was thunderstruck.

Since then, I think … well, I think that Maggie likes me.

2
Hooray for Monday!

Since Maggie came to our school about a month ago, everything has been different. I never liked school before. Now I wish there weren't any weekends. I get bored and I can't wait till Monday.

It's not because I love school-work. It's because of Maggie. I can't wait to see her. She might smile and wink at me. She often smiles and winks at me at recess.

I would like to smile and wink back, but I can't.

It's not that I'm embarrassed or shy. I just don't know how to wink.

It sounds stupid, but that's the way it is. I've been trying. I tried a million times, and I still can't do it.

At home I stand in front of the big mirror in the bathroom and scrunch up my face, this way and that, but it's no good. I can never wink.

It's as if my eyes were attached inside my head. When I close one, it pulls on the other and I look like a monster called the Cyclops that I saw once in a cartoon, with just one big eye in the middle of my forehead.

So instead of winking I just wave at Maggie. It's a lot easier and I'm sure she likes it just as much.

Maggie came to our school in the middle of the year. I don't know why. It doesn't matter anyway.

The important thing is that she's here, and I can see her.

She never speaks to me directly, but I know that she's interested in me. A little bird told me. And it must be true, because little

birds know all about this kind of thing.

I know that Maggie is there, not far away, and I know she likes me, and I can count on her. She's not in my class, but it's as if she was always around. Gary doesn't dare lay a finger on me. He knows what would happen if he did.

I only have only to close my eyes, and she's right beside me, with her long red hair. Then...

"What? I beg your pardon? Answer the question? What question?"

3
Beware! Jealous dog

But you haven't heard the best of it!

Mooch is jealous.

Not jealous of another dog, not jealous of the big cat next door, or of any other animal.

Mooch is jealous of Maggie.

And when I say jealous, I don't mean just ordinary jealousy. Mooch is *mad* with jealousy!

No way can I talk to her about Maggie. I can't even mention her name. She won't stand for it.

If I accidentally let it slip, Mooch throws a tantrum. She takes my slippers and chews them and tosses them around. She starts barking like a mad dog. She rolls in my comforter until it is covered with German Shepherd hairs.

She goes crazy!

She did exactly the same thing when my godmother came to visit with her poodle. Mooch was uncontrollable.

The only difference is that Maggie isn't like a poodle! Not a bit like a poodle! And Maggie hasn't set foot in our house.

I don't see what Mooch has against her. Maybe old age is getting to Mooch. All I know is it's not very funny.

Mooch doesn't even want to sleep next to my bed like she used to. She's sulking. She sleeps halfway into the closet so

I won't see her.

When a dog starts to act weird, it's unreal!

And all this because of a girl who never did anything to her! A girl she's never even seen!

Maybe Judy's right. Maybe we won't be able to keep Mooch much longer now that she's nine years old and acting really crazy.

4
Porcupine trouble

"You should have been watching her, Carl! You know how strange she's been lately."

"I was watching her, but she tore off into the woods. I couldn't get to her that fast. I only have two legs!"

"Help me hold her, anyway. We have to get these quills out as quickly as we can. We can't let her walk around like this."

"It's going to hurt. She won't like it."

"Just hold her front paws and I'll do it."

"You'll hurt her, Mom, I know

you will! We better take her to the vet."

"No way. If we take her to the vet, she'll start shaking like a leaf on a tree. I'll get these out in two seconds with my tweezers, you'll see. Hold her still now."

I tell you, Mooch was a sight to behold. Her nose looked like a pincushion. She had three quills stuck in her nose and one in her tongue.

What a great idea, to stick her nose into a porcupine.

You'd think she learned her lesson when she tangled with the skunk!

"Sit still, Mooch, and please lift your head, unless you want Judy to pull off one of your ears instead of these quills.

"Judy is not going to tweeze

your eyebrows, don't worry. She's just going to pull out those needles hanging from your nose.

"Good girl. Only two more left. Be a brave girl now and I'll give you a dog biscuit when Judy's finished."

"I don't understand how this happened, Carl. Normally she doesn't attack other animals.

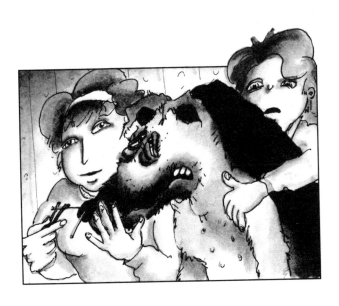

She just runs away. It looks like she tried to swallow the porcupine whole!"

"Maybe the porcupine surprised her. Maybe with her poor eyesight, she didn't see it."

"I think she's lost her wits."

If only I could tell Judy that the problem was really quite simple.

It all happened because of Maggie!

Stupid me, I said her name aloud while Mooch and I were walking in the woods. I just forgot.

That was all it took!

Yap, leap, growl! There was no holding her back.

She was off, dashing in all directions like a blown-up balloon with the air shooting out.

Then *bang*! Head first into a porcupine!

Boing! The quills hit the target. Or maybe I should say the target hit the quills.

And Mooch turned into the world's first dogupine!

And all because Miss Mooch is jealous. She's jealous of a twelve-year-old Viking with flaming red hair, wearing old jeans full of holes.

5
Schoolyard rumour

I don't know what's up this morning. I can't find Maggie anywhere. She's usually at school by this time.

Maybe she's sick, but I doubt it. That girl is so strong, no virus would have a chance against her.

Not like me. I catch any bug that comes within a hundred miles of me. Or rather, it catches me.

But any bug that wanted to catch Maggie would have to run pretty fast, or it would be left in the dust.

Maggie is just not the type to

get sick. I wonder where she can be.

"Looking for someone, Carl?"

"Mind your own business, Sebastian, unless you want —"

"If I were you, I'd start saying my prayers."

"Leave me alone, would you? You're just bugging me because Maggie isn't here yet, but just you wait."

"Oh, I guess little Carl doesn't know yet."

"Know what?"

"Your Maggie —"

"She's not MY Maggie!"

"She's gone!"

"Don't you wish!"

"She is gone! She's history! She's outa here!"

"What do you mean?"

"Everyone knows. Everyone but

you, I guess. But you're always a bit slow."

"Get a life!"

"Okay, okay. But just wait till Gary gets back. He's only gone for today."

"Why has Maggie left, know-it-all?"

"Because she's dumb. Just like your dog. Because she's twelve and she doesn't know how to write her own name. That's why"

"Liar! I'll write her name for you! I'll write it all over your face!"

6
Gary's going to get me

"Stop licking my eye. I know that's how dogs take care of themselves. But I'm not a dog, see? It won't make me feel better."

I don't need a St. Bernard to rescue me. I need a REAL German Shepherd!

Tomorrow, Gary will be back at school. He'll find out that Maggie has gone and that I got in a fight with his friend Sebastian. What's going to happen to me?

You're not answering, Mooch. You're flopping your ears down so you won't hear me.

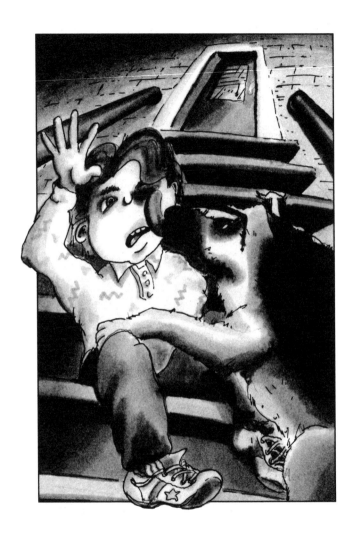

What's going to happen is I'm going to die. I'll be dead, do you hear me? Demolished. *Kaput*— that's German. You're a German Shepherd, Mooch. You must know German.

But no, all you know is that Maggie has gone and you've got nothing left to worry about. You're as happy as can be.

You don't care what happens to me now. It's all the same to you. You think that if you lick me a couple of times, I'll feel better.

Well, you're wrong.

Get that old wet rag of a tongue away from me. And keep your big fat hairy paw to yourself.

I need someone who understands. Maggie has gone and I'm sad.

I need someone who understands that Gary and his pals are waiting for me at school. I'm scared.

Someone who understands that nothing has changed. It's just the same as before Maggie was around.

I'm even lonelier now, because before I didn't even know Maggie existed.

All I've got now is an old, half-deaf, half-blind dog who's afraid of her own shadow, and who's looking at me and—

—and crying.

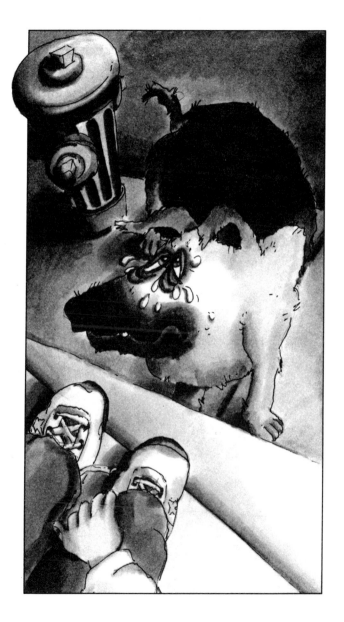

7
Sick and betrayed

We humans are not very bright. I would never have thought that a German Shepherd could have a nervous breakdown. Like my Aunt Alice.

This morning, Mooch didn't move. When I woke up, she was lying in the closet letting out little moans with every breath.

In fact, it started last night, after I told her about my problems at school, I called her all those names.

But this morning it was much worse. Mooch kept on moaning and she couldn't get up. It was as if her back legs were paralysed.

I told Judy right away and she called the vet over. He's the one who called it a nervous breakdown. Old age and depression.

He said it was normal at Mooch's age. A whole lot of little things can go wrong, but in Mooch's case there was more to it than that.

Judy mentioned that Mooch had been acting strange lately. The vet said that was probably the first sign of her breakdown.

He asked whether Mooch had had any bad experiences lately, whether she had been left alone a lot or kept away from us.

Judy said she hadn't, but I knew she had.

The whole time Maggie was at our school, I just ignored Mooch. I was with her, I was at home, but I was really somewhere else.

Everything Mooch did just bugged me. She got on my nerves. I didn't even want to have her around.

All I could think of was Maggie, and Mooch could tell. She could smell it in the air … feel it in her heart.

That's why she's sick now. Because, for a month, I forgot about all she had done for me for the last nine years and I just dropped her like a hot potato.

That's why she was crying

last night.

And that's why she could hardly stand up this morning.

She's been betrayed.

8
The case of the missing hamburger

Believe it or not, I'm still alive.

Gary came back to school, and nothing happened. He even told Sebastian to leave me alone.

Gary has changed.

Some people say it's because his dad came home. For years Gary told everybody that his dad was away on a trip.

One week he'd be in the United States, the next week he'd be in France. A month later, he'd be in Japan.

It was quite a trip!

I am not sure he really went so

far away. I think Gary might have been exaggerating a bit.

But I'm glad his dad is home now. For Gary's sake and mine.

We're both happier at school now.

I always thought that Gary didn't really like fighting all the time. That was just his way of showing that something inside was hurting him.

For the time being anyway, things are peaceful and that's great. At home, though, it's not so quiet.

Not because Mooch is still sick. Oh no!

Mooch is better now. Much better.

She managed to get on her feet the same day the vet came. He gave her a shot and it seemed to have a miraculous effect. I don't think it was really the shot. It's because I apologized. I think she really appreciated that.

I even begged her forgiveness.

Two minutes later she was up and about.

Dogs understand a lot more than we think. They have feelings, just like children.

Ever since then, Mooch has slept next to my bed. She sleeps so close, in fact, that half the time her tail is in my face and I have to put my pillow over my head so I won't hear her snoring.

But no problem. It's proof that Mooch has forgiven me.

And we also got proof that Mooch's nervous breakdown is

over. This afternoon, Judy spent ten minutes looking for the pound of hamburger she had left on the kitchen counter.

All she could find was a little piece of plastic wrap, right next to Mooch's water bowl!